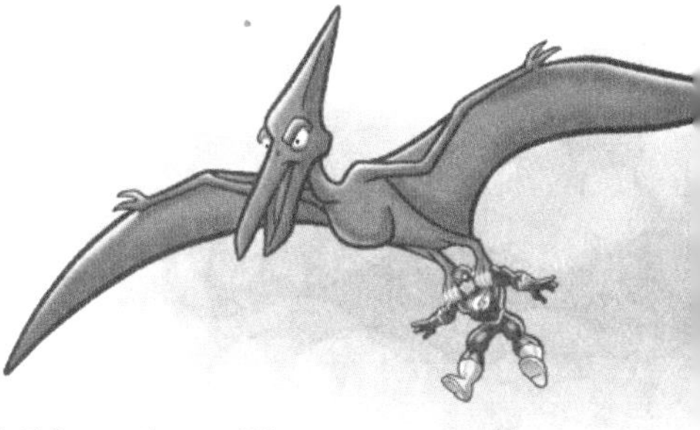

Dear Parent:

Congratulations! Your child is taking the first steps on an exciting journey. The destination? Independent reading!

STEP INTO READING® will help your child get there. The program offers five steps to reading success. Each step includes fun stories and colorful art. There are also Step into Reading Sticker Books, Step into Reading Math Readers, Step into Reading Phonics Readers, Step into Reading Write-In Readers, and Step into Reading Phonics Boxed Sets—a complete literacy program with something to interest every child.

Learning to Read, Step by Step!

STEP 1 Ready to Read **Preschool–Kindergarten**
• big type and easy words • rhyme and rhythm • picture clues
For children who know the alphabet and are eager to begin reading.

STEP 2 Reading with Help **Preschool–Grade 1**
• basic vocabulary • short sentences • simple stories
For children who recognize familiar words and sound out new words with help.

STEP 3 Reading on Your Own **Grades 1–3**
• engaging characters • easy-to-follow plots • popular topics
For children who are ready to read on their own.

STEP 4 Reading Paragraphs **Grades 2–3**
• challenging vocabulary • short paragraphs • exciting stories
For newly independent readers who read simple sentences with confidence.

STEP 5 Ready for Chapters **Grades 2–4**
• chapters • longer paragraphs • full-color art
For children who want to take the plunge into chapter books but still like colorful pictures.

STEP INTO READING® is designed to give every child a successful reading experience. The grade levels are only guides. Children can progress through the steps at their own speed, developing confidence in their reading, no matter what their grade.

Remember, a lifetime love of reading starts with a single step!

For Mom and Dad, and in memory of Joe Orlando
—E.D.
For Victor Paul
—D.S.

To Dad, who always encouraged me to draw
—M.D.

Visit us on the Web!
StepIntoReading.com
www.randomhouse.com/kids

Educators and librarians, for a variety of teaching tools, visit us at
www.randomhouse.com/teachers

ISBN: 978-0-375-86777-4 (trade)
ISBN: 978-0-375-96777-1 (lib. bdg.)

Printed in the United States of America   10 9 8 7 6 5 4 3 2 1

T. REX TROUBLE!

By Dennis "Rocket" Shealy

Illustrated by Erik Doescher,

Mike DeCarlo, and David Tanguay

Random House 🏠 New York

Dinosaur fossils
are on parade.

Lex Luthor has a plan.

He sprays the T. Rex

with his super foam.

Foam covers the bones.
The T. rex comes to life!

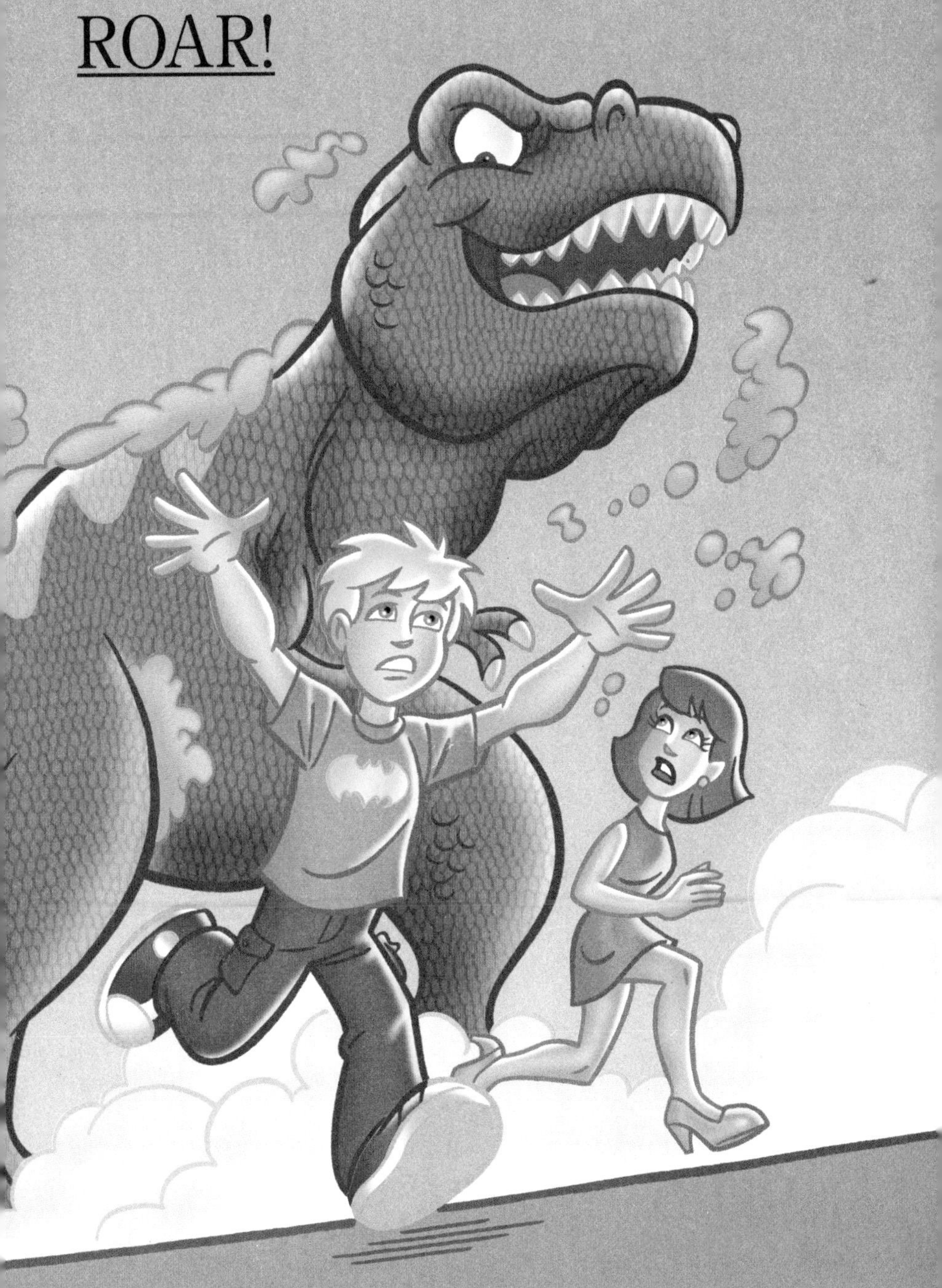
ROAR!

Lex rides the T. rex.
He makes more dinosaurs
come to life.

The pteranodon flies!

The triceratops stomps!

Flash sees the dinosaurs.

He calls the Super Friends.

The pteranodon
grabs Flash.

Flash cannot get away.

The dinosaurs
scare the people.

Lex takes their money
and valuables.

The Super Friends arrive.

Batman says,

"Stop right there!"

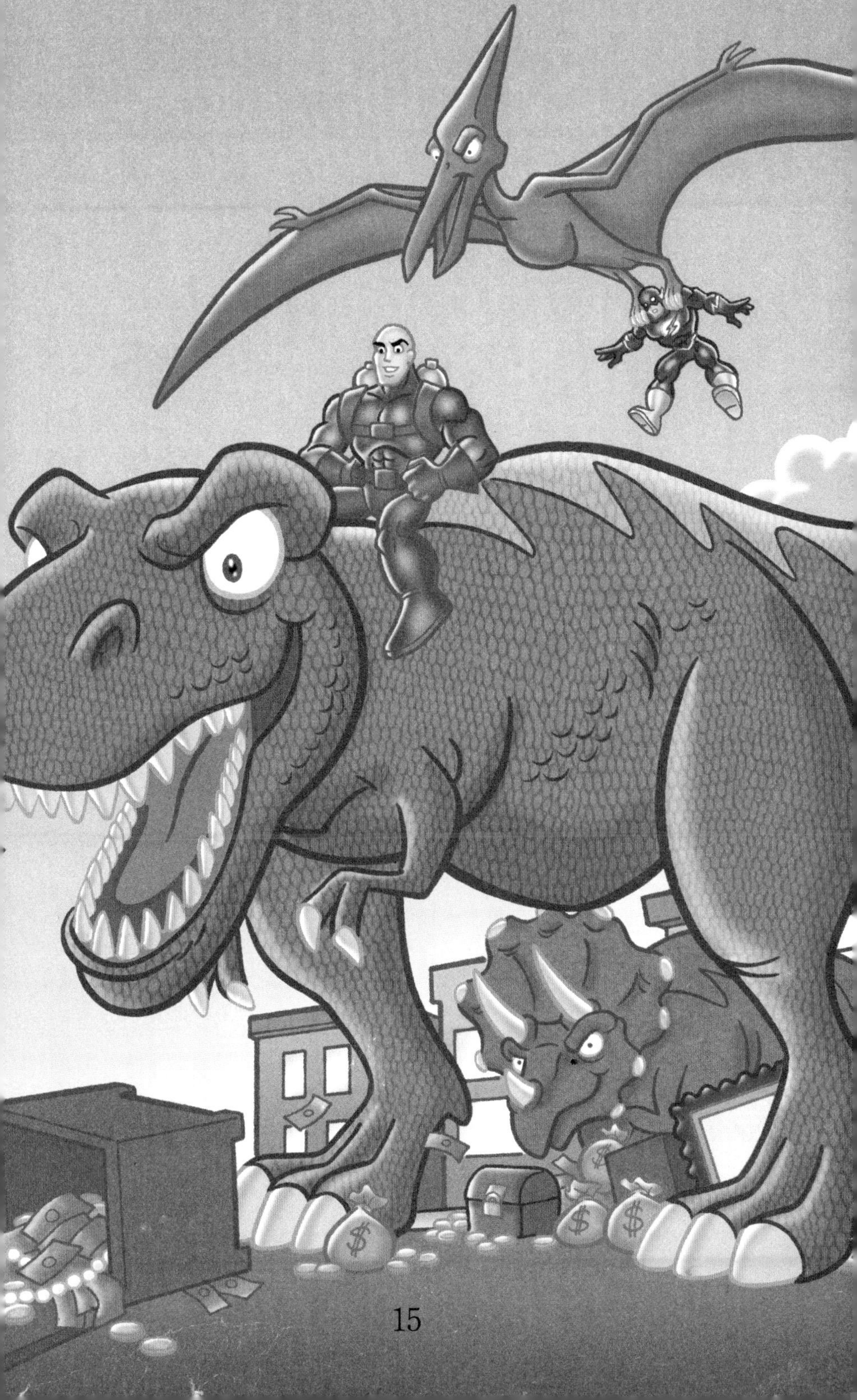

Lex orders the dinosaurs
to attack.

The dinosaurs charge
at the Super Friends!

Batman lassos

the triceratops.

The dinosaur bucks.
Batman holds on tight!

Green Lantern saves
Flash with a tornado.

Green Lantern sets Flash
safely on the ground.

Superman fights
the T. rex.
Its mouth is
full of sharp teeth!

Superman keeps its jaws
from snapping shut!

Batman sees
a grocery truck.
He has an idea.

Batman steers
the triceratops
into the truck.

Meat and fish
pour out of the truck.

The dinosaurs
run to the food.

The pteranodon and
the T. rex start to eat.

Flash grabs Lex!

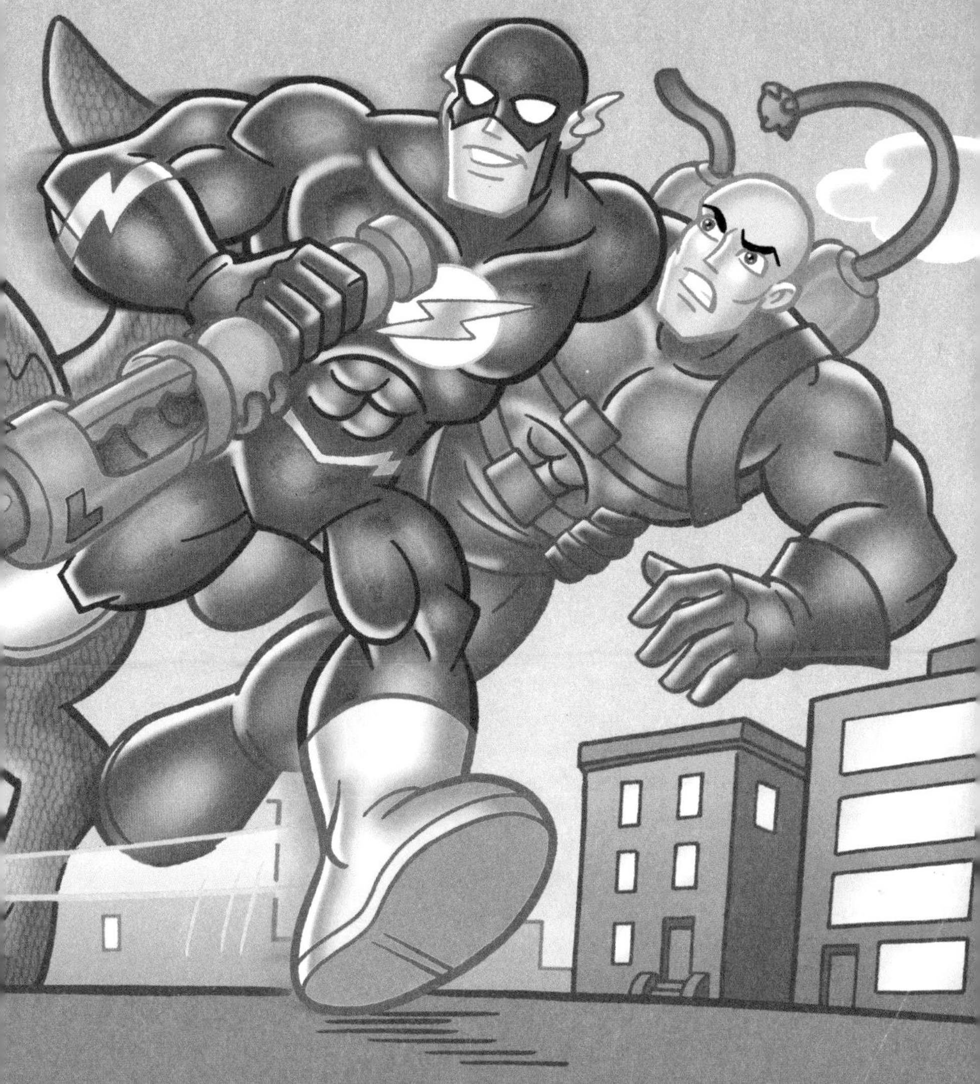

Lex's plan has failed.
The Super Friends
have made friends
with the dinosaurs!

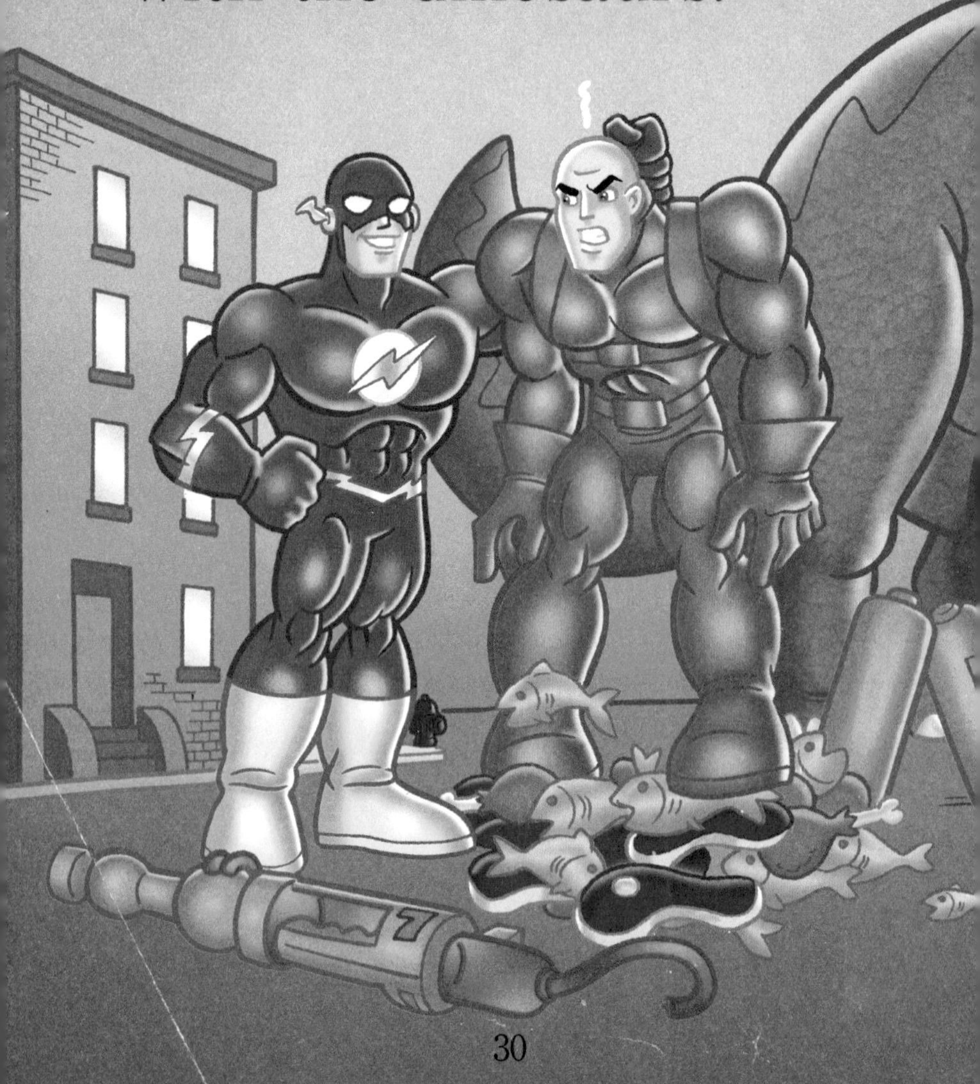

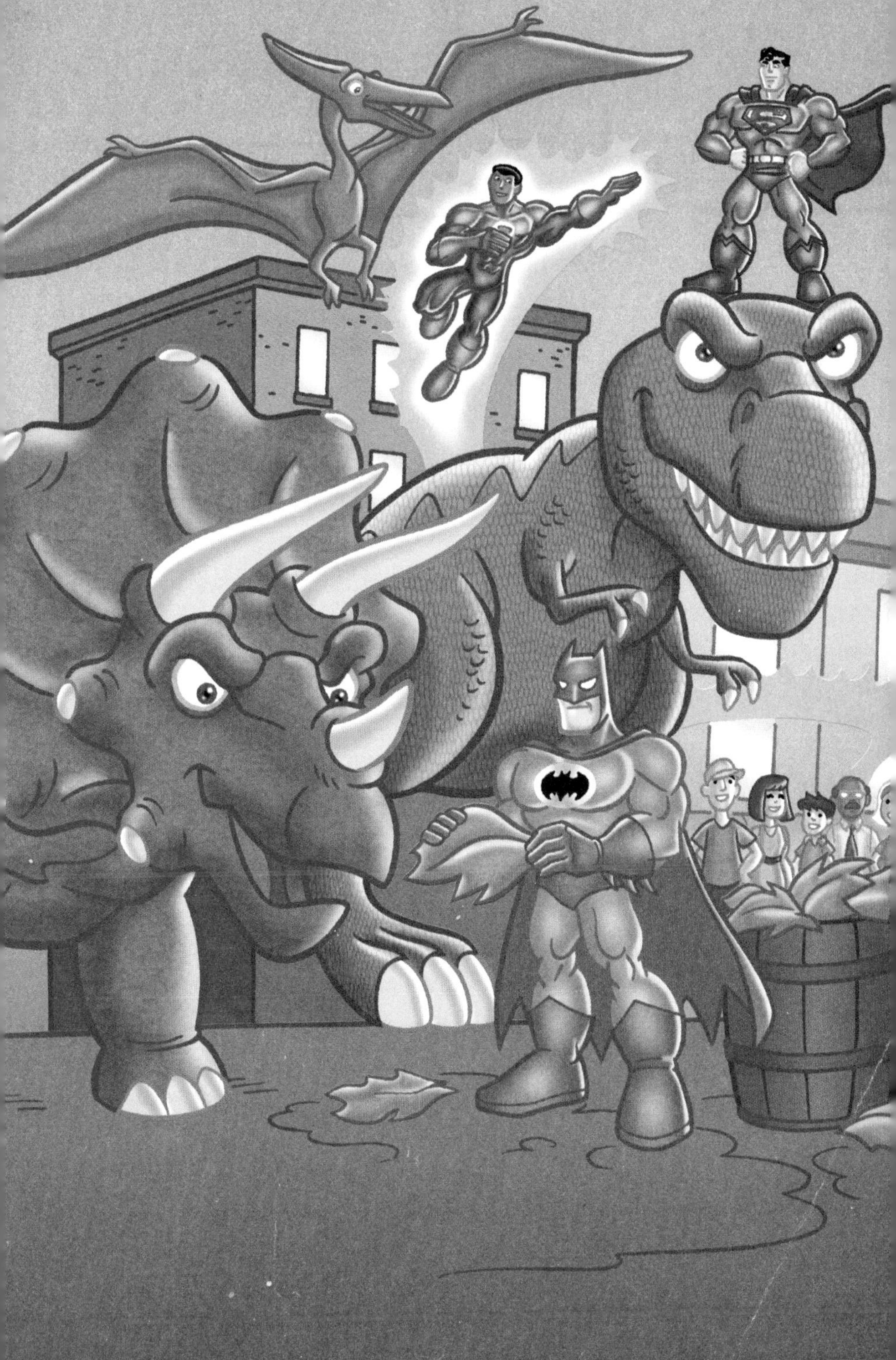

The Super Friends build
a home for the dinosaurs.
Everyone cheers!